Parent's Introduction

We Both Read is the first series of b͏ ͏invite parents and children to share the reading of a aloud. This "shared reading" innovati reading education specialists, invites pa text and storyline on the left-hand pages. ͏to read the right-hand pages, which feature less co specifically written for the beginning reader.

Reading aloud is one of the most important activities parents can share with their child to assist them in their reading development. However, *We Both Read* goes beyond reading *to* a child and allows parents to share the reading *with* a child. *We Both Read* is so powerful and effective because it combines two key elements in learning: "modeling" (the parent reads) and "doing" (the child reads). The result is not only faster reading development for the child, but a much more enjoyable and enriching experience for both!

You may find it helpful to read the entire book aloud yourself the first time, then invite your child to participate in the second reading. In some books, a few more difficult words will first be introduced in the parent's text, distinguished with **bold lettering**. Pointing out, and even discussing, these words will help familiarize your child with them and help to build your child's vocabulary. Also, note that a "talking parent" icon ☺ precedes the parent's text and a "talking child" icon ☺ precedes the child's text.

We encourage you to share and interact with your child as you read the book together. If your child is having difficulty, you might want to mention a few things to help them. "Sounding out" is good, but it will not work with all words. Children can pick up clues about the words they are reading from the story, the context of the sentence, or even the pictures. Some stories have rhyming patterns that might help. It might also help them to touch the words with their finger as they read, to better connect the voice sound and the printed word.

Sharing the *We Both Read* books together will engage you and your child in an interactive adventure in reading! It is a fun and easy way to encourage and help your child to read—and a wonderful way to start them off on a lifetime of reading enjoyment!

We Both Read: The Well-Mannered Monster

We Both Read® is a registered trademark of Treasure Bay, Inc.

Published by Treasure Bay, Inc.
40 Sir Francis Drake Boulevard
San Anselmo, CA 94960 USA

PRINTED IN SINGAPORE

Library of Congress Catalog Card Number: 2005905160

Hardcover ISBN-10: 1-891327-65-8
Hardcover ISBN-13: 978-1-891327-65-0
Paperback ISBN-10: 1-891327-66-6
Paperback ISBN-13: 978-1-891327-66-7

We Both Read® Books
Patent No. 5,957,693

Visit us online at:
www.webothread.com

The
Well-Mannered
Monster

By Marcy Brown and Dennis Haley

Illustrated by Tim Raglin

TREASURE BAY

My name is Pat and this is Matt. He is my very best friend in the whole world. He also just happens to be a **monster.**

He is a big **monster** and he is a fun **monster**.

I like being best friends with Matt. Even though he is a monster, he has very good **manners.** When we play with our friends, Matt makes sure everyone gets a chance to play.

He takes turns. Taking turns is good **manners.**

Matt always plays fair and never breaks the rules. Sometimes he wins. Sometimes he doesn't. If he doesn't win, he is still happy to have played and is never a poor sport.

That is why it is fun to play with Matt.

One day my mother was making a very special dinner. There were pots and pans and plates everywhere. She was working very hard, so Matt **asked** if we **could** help.

Mom said, "Yes." She **asked** if we **could** go to the store for her.

Mom gave us a list of what she needed. She reminded us that it was a long way to the store. We were going to have to cross the street. Matt said we **would** be very careful.

Matt said he **would** hold
my hand. He always does
when we cross the street.

On the way we saw my mailman, Mr. Bell. I said "Hello," and Matt said, "Hello," too. He waved as big as he could, but Mr. Bell did not wave back.

Mr. Bell did not know
Matt. He had never met
a monster.

Matt knew the polite thing to do was to introduce himself. He told Mr. Bell that his name was Matt and that it was nice to **meet** him. Then he shook his hand.

Mr. Bell was happy to **meet** Matt. He was glad to know his name.

After we saw Mr. Bell, we saw a lady standing outside of the store. She was carrying such a big box that she could not **open** the door by herself. Matt knew just what to do.

He **opened** the door for her. "**After** you," he said.

In the store was a man who wanted a box of soap. It was way up high on the top shelf. He tried to reach it, but he couldn't.

So Matt and I helped him.
It is good to help if you can.
You can help if you are big
or small.

After we were done shopping, we met the store owner. He said he had been worried about having a monster in his store, but he was not worried anymore.

He said that Matt was a very nice monster. He was happy to have Matt shop at his store.

On our way home, we saw our friend, Rose. She wanted us to play ball. We thanked her, but said we had **promised** to go straight home.

We gave our word to Mom. We were going to keep our **promise.**

Dinner was ready. Matt and I helped to bring out the food. By the time we were finished, there was so much food it covered the whole table.

It was a lot of food,
even for a monster!

The doorbell rang and Matt answered it. There were lots of **people** at the door! There were our neighbors and our mailman, Mr. Bell. Mom had invited all of them over for dinner.

We had lots of food. We had lots of **people**. Now we could have dinner!

I helped people with their chairs. Mom gave everyone fresh ice water. Matt put his napkin on his lap and didn't take a bite until everyone had their food.

Manners are nice. They show people that you care.

Sometimes, even after everyone has their food, they need one more thing. Matt needed **butter** for his bread. He knew he could reach across the table for it, but he decided to say **"please"** instead.

He asked Mr. Bell to **please** pass the **butter**. Then he said, "Thank you."

Mr. Bell said, "You are welcome."

When anyone spoke to Matt, he listened with both of his ears. He waited until they were done **talking** before he spoke. He did not ever interrupt.

All of us like to **talk**.
It is good to take turns.

Finally my mom brought out dessert. She had used the sugar we bought to make chocolate chip **cookies**! She'd made a special one for Matt!

Matt said, "Thank you." He likes **cookies**. He likes big **cookies** even more.

Even if your food tastes great, no one wants to see it in your mouth. I always try to keep my **mouth** closed while I am eating.

Matt does too. He does not talk with his **mouth** full and he uses his napkin.

All the guests thanked my mom, Matt and me for a wonderful dinner. We said, "You're welcome." Then Matt and I thanked my mother in our own way, by **helping** to wash the dishes.

Helping is another way to say, "Thank you." It can be fun too!

Before we went to sleep, Matt wrote a thank-you note to my mother for his special cookie. Then he thanked me for making him a part of such a wonderful day. He really is a nice and well-mannered monster.

That is why I like him.

If you liked
The Well-Mannered Monster, **here are two other**
We Both Read® **Books you are sure to enjoy!**

The young boy, Kibu, lives in Africa and is a member of the Masai tribe. When Kibu is told he is too small to go on the lion hunt, he decides to prove that he too can be a mighty lion hunter. With a basket of food from his mother he sets out into the African wilderness to find the biggest lion of all, Father Lion. With the help of some animal friends, Kibu hopes to outsmart Father Lion and return victorious.